S0-BRB-830

RYE FREE READING ROOM

PLANET IN CRISIS

WASTE MANAGEMENT CRISIS

This edition published in 2009 by:
The Rosen Publishing Group, Inc.
29 East 21st Street
New York, NY 10010

Designed and produced by
David West Books

Editor: James Pickering
Picture Research: Carlotta Cooper

Photo Credits: Abbreviations: t-top, m-middle, b-bottom, r-right,
l-left, c-center.

Front cover, r & 4r - Corbis Images. 3 & 16–17, 22l (David Drain); 5r (Hellier Mason); 6t, (Mark Edwards);
9tl (Sabine Vielmo); 9tr, 18–19 (Matt Meadows); 10t (Wehrmann/UNEP); 11b (Aaron Jacobs); 13t, 27b
(Dylan Garcia); 14t, 21mb (David Hoffman); 15m (Andre Maslennikov); 17t (Remy Steinegger) - World
Economic Forum; 18–19t (Herbert Giradet); 18, 30 (Hartmut Schwarzbach); 21ml, 24, 25tl (Ray Pfortner);
21t (Cryptome); 22r (Don Riepe); 25tr (ToastyKen); 27t (Ceanne Jansen) - Still Pictures. 5b & 10–11 (Sipa
Press); 6b (Tony Kyriacou); 10b (Veronica Garbutt); 11m (Nicholas Bailey); 12b, 21br (Action Press); 13b
(William F. Campbell/ TimePix); 15b (KellyK); 16 (Peter Brooker); 17m (Brendan Beirne); 19b Startech; 23b
(Tschaen); 25b (Michael L. Abramson/TimePix); 28–29t (Isopress Senepart); 6-7, 8b, 14b, 23t & m, 26m, 28
- Rex Features Ltd. 7b, 12–13, 26b, 28–29b - Corbis Images. 23br - © 2003 EcoReefs, Inc; 29b
(urbanwoodswalker).

Library of Congress Cataloging-in-Publication Data

Parker, Russ, 1970-
Waste management crisis / Russ Parker.
    p. cm. -- (Planet in crisis)
Includes bibliographical references and index.
ISBN 978-1-4358-5253-2 (library binding) -- ISBN 978-1-4358-0683-2 (pbk.) -- ISBN 978-1-4358-0689-4
(6-pack)
1. Refuse and refuse disposal--Juvenile literature. 2. Waste minimization--Juvenile literature. 3. Hazardous
waste--Juvenile literature. I. Title.
TD792.P369 2009
363.72'85--dc22

                                    2008043727

Printed and bound in China

First published in Great Britain by Heinemann Library, a division of Reed Educational and Professional Publishing Limited.

PLANET IN CRISIS

WASTE MANAGEMENT CRISIS

Russ Parker

rosen publishing's
rosen central

New York

CONTENTS

The more tons of paper and other substances we recycle, the less it costs per ton, and the greater the savings in materials, time, and energy.

The official symbols for reuse and recycling that appear on products and materials remind us to avoid creating unnecessary waste.

Hot topic
Traffic jams are not only irritating and time-consuming, they also waste vast amounts of precious, irreplaceable resources—especially gas and other fuels, which literally go up in smoke.

Going nowhere wastefully

NOT ENOUGH

People in developed nations expect to enjoy comfortable lifestyles. Some see attempts to cut waste and increase recycling as threats to their comfortable way of life. People in developing places lack money for cars, consumer goods, fast food meals, and other products. Their lifestyles are simpler and less wasteful, but they are also uncomfortable and full of hardship. Many of these people hope that they will soon achieve a wealthy lifestyle. In one sense, their aim is to have enough money to be as wasteful as the developed nations.

Many products are made of plastics, and most plastics come from oil or petroleum, which is processed at huge refineries. Some experts predict that at our current rate of use, oil will run out in less than a hundred years.

8 CATEGORIES OF WASTE

Different types of wastes are treated, recycled, or disposed of in different ways. It is vital to sort wastes into groups.

MAJOR TYPES OF WASTE

Main categories of wastes for recycling include:
- Paper, posterboard, and cardboard.
- Clothing and textiles, natural and artificial.
- Various types of plastics, like ABS and PET.
- Glass, usually sorted by color.
- Metals, including iron, steel, and aluminum.
- Organic wastes such as vegetable peels, rotten fruit, and leftover food.

Sealed barrels are used to store radioactive waste. These have to be handled very carefully by people in protective clothing, which then becomes contaminated as "low level" waste.

After plastics and other materials are removed from old cars, their bodies can be melted down for recycling at the steel factory.

Toxic wastes include chemicals like acids which are dangerous, harmful, or poisonous. They are clearly labeled for workers' safety.

POISON

Contaminated wastes from hospitals and laboratories may carry germs or disease. They might be small in volume, but they need careful attention.

METAL WASTE

Ferrous metals are those based on iron, including many kinds of steels used for canned foods, car bodies, and domestic appliances. These can be recycled via scrapyards back into the steel furnaces. Aluminum is a softer, lightweight metal used for drink cans, tin foils, and food cartons. It is one of the most successfully recycled substances.

Hot topic

New technologies, gadgets, and inventions bring different types of waste. They also create new opportunities to recycle, especially in fast-moving areas such as computing and electronics.

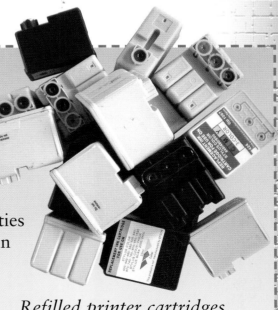

Refilled printer cartridges

If each person or household had to dispose of waste separately, this would cause huge problems. In most places, the local city or town (municipality) organizes collections of garbage, refuse, and waste, from houses, schools, and smaller offices and businesses.

A LOCAL SERVICE

Household waste makes up between one-half and two-thirds of municipal waste. The collections are usually paid for by local taxes, which also fund schools, libraries, roads, and other services. More recycling and less waste mean more to spend on these other services.

Hot topic

Putting different types of wastes into different bags or containers is vital—and with a sensible system, it soon becomes a habit. Bags are put in convenient, easily accessible places near where the waste is produced.

"Sorting at source," Germany

Waste reduction can start before products reach the home, by choosing those with minimal or recyclable packaging (left). This greatly helps relieve pressure on landfills (below).

HOW MUCH RUBBISH?

In general, richer and more industrialized nations throw out more waste per person than less developed countries. In an industrialized country, an average person is responsible for their own body weight in waste every six to eight weeks. One-fifth of this is paper and cardboard, which is almost all recyclable.

SORTING AT SOURCE

To recycle municipal waste efficiently, a key feature is "sorting at source." This means putting different types of waste into different bags, bins, or containers from the very beginning. Otherwise garbage cans and trash bags contain mixed waste which must be sorted later—a process that is costly, difficult, dirty, and even dangerous. Local governments and city or township sanitation departments help us to do this as easily as possible. For example, they can provide clearly marked and color-coded containers or bins in convenient places for the main different types of waste.

Door-to-door or curbside collection is one method of gathering waste. Recycling bins or containers are also put in many public places for paper, glass, and other materials. Malls, parking lots, stadiums, and other places can also have recycling facilities.

When we consider the tons of waste we produce, we are only thinking about "after" waste—after goods and products are used. A key issue in developed countries is what happens "before?"

THE "WASTE CHAIN"

Waste is produced along the whole chain of industry, from obtaining raw materials and their transportation, to making products in factories and distributing them to stores.

Production of organic water pollutants

7,000
6,000
5,000
4,000
3,000
2,000
1,000

Tons per day

China
U.S.
India
Russia
Japan
Indonesia
Germany
Ukraine
UK
France

WATER-POLLUTING WASTES

Some wastes are not obvious. They are liquids which wash away into the water system of drains, rivers, lakes, and oceans. But they can cause huge problems, especially pollution.

Industrial chemicals 15%

Others 6%

Textiles 14%

Wastewater pollutants harm fish and other wildlife, soak into soil, and contaminate farm crops and animals. Cleanups cost time and money—and make more waste.

Paper and pulp **10%**

Metals **12%**

Agricultural chemicals **3%**

Food and drink production **40%**

Water pollutants by type of industry

Hot topic
New cars are not quite so wasteful compared to older ones. They use less fuel, produce fewer harmful gases, and contain more parts for recycling when the car reaches the end of the road.

Newer cars are "greener."

SPECIAL PROBLEMS

Each type of industry has its own special waste problems. For example, making paper and processing foods and drinks require vast quantities of water which should then be treated and cleaned after use. Metal production uses huge amounts of energy to melt the ores (metal-bearing rocks), and the leftovers, or slags, pile up into tall mountains that ruin the landscape.

Holes and waste piles from old quarries and mines.

13

Piles of plastic and rusty metal pose many waste disposal problems. But other types of wastes can be far more dangerous to our own health, and to life and survival around the globe. Two of these categories are toxic and nuclear wastes.

Toxic wastes are usually dealt with at special storage facilities or treatment plants, usually by adding other chemicals, which make them less harmful.

TOXIC WASTES

Toxins are substances that are poisonous or harmful to humans and other living things. Some are useful because of this ability. For example, some toxins kill crop-infesting pests. Others are by-products of industry. Toxic wastes must be safely contained, clearly identified, and carefully handled at every stage of their disposal. If they spill or escape, they can cause widespread, long-lasting harm.

Toxic wastes are a hazard even during transport. These experts are cleaning up a chemical spill after a road accident.

SAFELY STORED?

Nuclear wastes must be stored, which creates huge problems. One new plan is to enclose nuclear wastes in strong containers or canisters buried in chambers deep under Yucca Mountain in Nevada. But could an earthquake release the radiation into the air or water, so a vast area becomes radioactive?

Radioactive wastes stored underground will need regular checks for leaks and other dangers, far into the future.

Yucca Mountain

Canister

High level waste

Storage chambers

Access tunnel

NUCLEAR WASTES

Nuclear material is one of the great problems of waste disposal. Most comes from nuclear power stations, as spent (used) fuel, equipment, and clothing. These give off invisible but harmful radioactivity, or radiation, which can cause serious illness or even death—and will last hundreds of years. At present, nuclear waste cannot be made safe or neutralized.

Hot topic

Picher, in Oklahoma, has an unwanted claim—it's one of the country's most polluted places. Nearby, at Tar Creek, are huge heaps of rock and dust from years of lead and zinc mining. The "Superfund" program for sites polluted with toxic waste is involved in the cleanup. To add to Picher's problems, a tornado there in March 2008 killed six people.

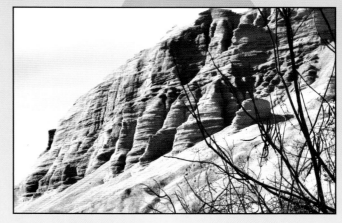

Picher's mounds of toxic mining waste.

In a developed country, each person is responsible each year for a pile of waste that would almost fill their own house. What happens to it?

FOUR FATES FOR WASTE

There are four main ways to deal with waste. It can be left in piles at dumps. It can be burned in incinerators or buried in landfills, as shown on the following pages. Last, and by far best, it can be recycled.

Burning vehicle tires releases dense smoke and toxic fumes. An alternative is to shred the rubber for recycling. But the strengthening metal cords within the rubber make this difficult and costly.

WHAT HAPPENS TO THEIR WASTE?

Different countries dispose of their waste in different ways. Nations with many people in a small area avoid burying, since they do not have enough land. They may choose incineration instead. The amounts recycled vary from less than one-twentieth to over one-third, but are growing everywhere.

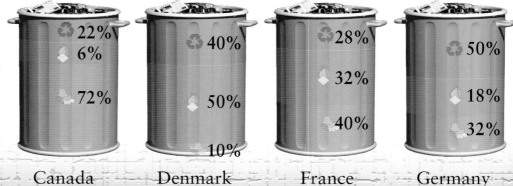

Canada	Denmark	France	Germany
22%	40%	28%	50%
6%		32%	
72%	50%	40%	18%
	10%		32%

Hot topic
Leaders and experts gather often to discuss global problems such as hunger, poverty, and waste. Famous speakers like former U.S. vice president Al Gore and musician Bono attract great media attention.

Bono and Al Gore meet at the 2008 World Economic Forum.

LEFT IN PILES
Piling up waste at open landfills or dumps is a huge danger. It attracts animals like flies and rats that spread disease. It creates horrific smells. Rain washes hazardous chemicals from it to pollute surrounding land and waterways.

Birds, rats, foxes, and other animals risk diseases as they scavenge at landfills —and so, in some countries, do people.

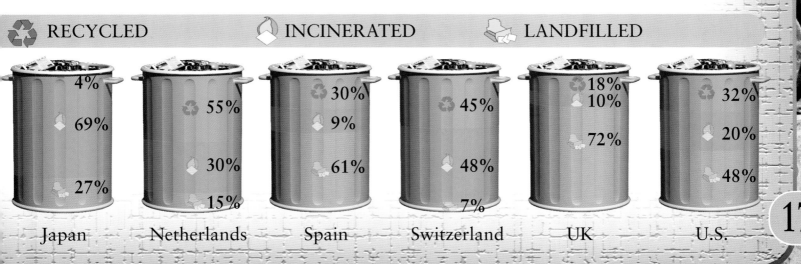

♻ RECYCLED   ◊ INCINERATED   🗑 LANDFILLED

	RECYCLED	INCINERATED	LANDFILLED
Japan	4%	69%	27%
Netherlands	55%	30%	15%
Spain	30%	9%	61%
Switzerland	45%	48%	7%
UK	18% / 10%	72%	
U.S.	32%	20%	48%

Burning waste might seem like a good idea. It gets rid of bulk and gives off heat energy to generate electricity or warm local buildings. But in practice, it involves many difficulties, and any burning contributes to global warming.

HARMFUL FUMES

Burning substances like rubber gives off thick, dark smoke which blackens the air and settles as dirty dust nearby. When some plastics burn, they release poisonous chemicals such as dioxins. So the smoke and fumes must be carefully filtered and cleaned.

Waste recycling plants burn garbage (above). Fumes are passed through scrubbers to remove harmful substances.

Generators that can make power from waste are expensive. Large amounts of garbage have to be sorted before being burnt (right).

Special incinerators for specific kinds of waste, like tires, are becoming more common. The burn temperature and time, and the filters and other equipment, are all designed to give off the least fumes and leave the least amount of ash.

HAZARDOUS REMAINS

Incinerators usually burn wastes at very high temperatures, 1,000°F or above. This leaves less ash and other leftover materials, which are usually buried in landfill sites. But unless the wastes are sorted beforehand, the ash and leftovers may contain toxic substances. These could leak from the landfill and become another source of harmful pollution.

Hot topic

A plasma converter changes solid waste into vapor using a continuous lightning-like spark from a plasma torch at 30,000°F. Metals and similar substances must be removed before vaporizing.

Experimental plasma converter

In many countries, especially those with lots of land to spare, most waste is buried. It's tipped into big holes called landfills and covered. It may be out of sight—but it isn't out of mind.

LANDFILL RISKS

Burying waste in a bare hole is very hazardous. Rain soaks in through the covering earth. It washes polluting chemicals into the surrounding soil, killing plants and animals. Streams carry the pollution into rivers and lakes.

LEACHATE AND METHANE

In a modern landfill site, this polluted water mixture, called leachate, is kept in by clay and other linings. It is sucked up by pipes and stored in tanks, for safe disposal later. As food and other materials rot, they give off the gas methane—which may explode. So this is also collected by pipes, to burn for heating or to generate electricity.

SAFER BURIAL

Layers of waste alternate with sand and gravel to allow water and gas to flow. Watery leachate is sucked from the bottom up through pipes to a tank. Methane gas is also led along pipes to burn and generate electricity.

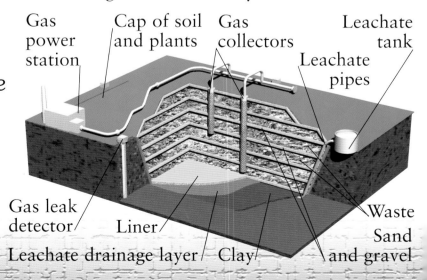

Gas power station

Cap of soil and plants

Gas collectors

Leachate tank

Leachate pipes

Gas leak detector

Liner

Leachate drainage layer

Clay

Waste

Sand and gravel

New York City's Fresh Kills Landfill, once the world's biggest, received 100,000 tons of trash weekly (above). In 2007, a 30-year plan began to turn it into a 2,200-acre park.

Equipment measures the amounts of methane and other gases.

Sites are capped with soil, grass, and young trees.

The site of the explosion.

21

Seas and oceans look endless, with plenty of room for dumping waste which will float away or sink to the bottom. But for too long, they have been used as the world's watery trash can.

DUMPED IN THE DEEP

Dumping waste at sea can be deadly. Salt water eats away, or corrodes, any containers and releases chemicals they contain. Waves, tides, and ocean currents spread the wastes far and wide, causing harm to fish, seals, seabirds, and other ocean life.

Too many people break the law by dumping garbage and waste in the wrong places. This is dangerous, spoils scenery, and causes pollution (above). Nearby soil and water must be checked for toxins (right).

HARMFUL TO HUMANS

Poisonous or toxic wastes move not only through water, but also through living things. They spread into a lake or ocean and are taken up with nutrients by small plants and animals.

1 Drum of toxic chemicals is dumped in lake or ocean.

2 Drum corrodes and leaks.

3 Plankton (tiny plants and animals) take in toxins.

4 Fish eat plankton.

5 Fish are caught and eaten.

Small living things are food for larger ones, like fish. The amounts of toxins increase in their bodies, along the food chain, to poison larger creatures like dolphins—or people.

Dumping wastes at sea is now against the law in many regions. This is partly due to direct action campaigns, where conservationists use boats to obstruct dumping ships and gain publicity.

Old oil rigs are a big waste problem. One suggestion is to sink them to the sea bed as sheltering places for creatures to live and breed (see below).

ON THE OPEN OCEAN

Because lakes and oceans are so big, people may dump wastes in the hope they cannot be traced. But modern technology helps to catch the criminals. Boats are tracked and photographed by satellites. Computers can work out how winds and currents move slicks of oil or chemicals, to reveal where the slick was originally dumped in the water.

Being GREEN

Shipwrecks teem with fish, crabs, and other life, thriving in the nooks and crannies. The same could happen to deliberately sunk ships, oil rigs, cars, or similar items, once they are cleaned of chemicals and other dangers. The Texas "rigs to reefs" program was begun in 1990 to dispose of old, unwanted oil rigs.

Dumped cars could be used to grow coral reefs (inset).

More than half of the waste we throw away at home could be recycled. To be effective, this should be a regular habit.

LESS WASTE ALL AROUND

"Sorting at source" (see page 11) makes recycling hundreds of times less costly than sorting out a bag or bin of mixed garbage later, which simply causes more waste—of time, energy, and money.

TALKING TRASH

A typical household produces about five main types of wastes. Food leftovers, fruit pits, vegetable peels, old flowers, and other scraps should not even be in the garbage can. They can be put into a compost heap to rot gradually and enrich the soil.

It only takes a minute or two on a weekly basis to sort household waste for a quick and easy collection.

Being GREEN

Communal compost heaps are popular in cities. Grass clippings, old leaves, plant trimmings, flower cuttings, and many other organic wastes are shredded and mixed in regularly. The greater the variety of wastes, the faster they rot or decay.

10% Natural materials (wood, leather, cotton, etc.)

10% Plastics

10% Glass

10% Metals

30% Paper and cardboard

30% Food leftovers and scraps

Communal compost

GET INTO THE HABIT

Once waste is sorted, it can be left for the regular collection. Or it can be taken to the local recycling centers, usually as part of another errand such as going to the supermarket. Making a special recycling trip in a car uses up fuel, and if time is short, it's more likely to be "forgotten."

Look for the recycling symbol on all products. Recycling bins are usually provided free to residents, as in San Francisco (above). Advice about recycling is also free!

House-to-house collection for recycling is more cost-effective in cities and towns than in rural areas.

25

... are not waste, but valuable raw materials. Some people say it is too inconvenient to recycle them. Yet Switzerland and Germany recycle four-fifths of their glass products.

HOW TO SAVE A RAINFOREST

For the metal aluminum, used to make soft drink cans, this recycling proportion is even higher—over nine-tenths in some countries. This saves four-fifths of the energy used to make new aluminum. It also saves tropical forests, since much of the ore rocks used for cans come from tropical regions.

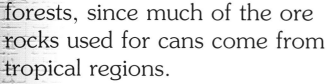

EVERY ALUMINIUM CAN YOU DROP IN HERE RAISES MONEY FOR

Imperial Cancer Research Fund

PLEASE HELP!

THIS INITIATIVE IS SUPPORTED BY:
Camden

Recycle Aluminium Cans

alu

EVERY ALUMINIUM CAN YOU DROP IN HERE RAISES MONEY FOR

Imperial Cancer Research Fund

PLEASE HELP!

THIS INITIATIVE IS SUPPORTED BY:
Camden

Aluminum recycling programs can be set up locally and used to raise funds for a neighborhood project. Every can is worth money!

Hot topic
A problem area for recycling is fast-advancing technical equipment, such as computers. They contain many different materials. But modern recycling centers can extract many of these.

Old computers for recycling

Metals are sorted at the scrapyard and then squashed under huge pressure into bales. This saves space for their trip to the steel factory by truck, train, or ship.

SAVINGS AT EVERY STAGE

Glass is another substance made using huge amounts of energy. Its raw materials are heated in furnaces to over 2,200°F. Recycling glass saves more than one-quarter of this energy. This means not only savings in the fuel used, such as coal or gas, but also fewer of the pollutants and greenhouse gases (which contribute to global warming) produced by burning that fuel.

Glass does not have to be crushed and melted in a furnace to be recycled. Unbroken bottles and jars can be cleaned and refilled several times.

27

Paper is made from trees. So recycling it saves not only trees, but also forest animals, huge amounts of energy, and great quantities of water.

MUST TRY HARDER

It should be possible to recycle over four-fifths of all paper and board. But around the world, the average is about one-half. We can help by taking more paper and cardboard to recycling centers and by choosing recycled paper products, from notepads to toilet paper.

Some of these crates and containers, already made from recycled plastic, will be recycled again into more basic items—such as traffic cones.

NEW PAPER FROM OLD

Paper from recycling bins is usually a mixture of different qualities or grades, from shiny new magazines to scrap newspaper. A common process is to shred it, mix it with water and chemicals into a mushy pulp, and press it into sheets, which dry to make recycled paper for packaging.

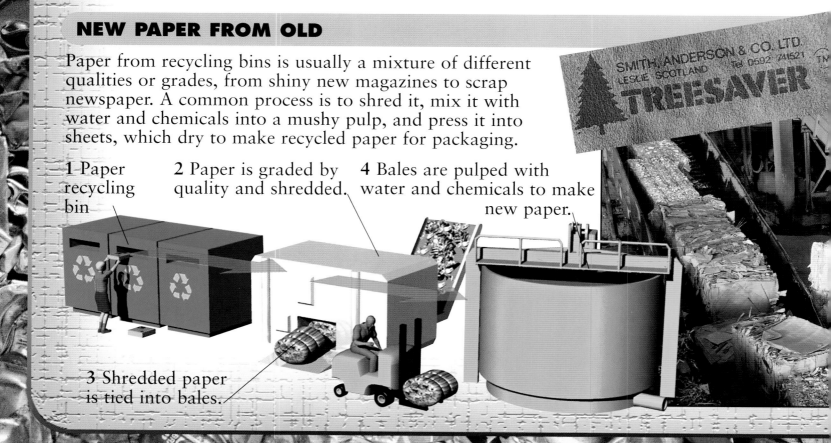

1 Paper recycling bin

2 Paper is graded by quality and shredded.

3 Shredded paper is tied into bales.

4 Bales are pulped with water and chemicals to make new paper.

SMITH, ANDERSON & CO. LTD.
LESLIE SCOTLAND   Tel 0592 741521   TM
TREESAVER

FAST PROGRESS

Plastics have been around for less than a hundred years. The technology for recycling them is even more recent, and it is growing fast. One reason is that most plastics are made from petroleum or oil. This natural resource, also used for fuels such as gasoline, is very valuable and limited—used at today's rates, it may run out by the year 2100. Common items for recycling are drinks bottles, made from the plastic PET.

Recycled paper requires, on average, only half the energy used to make new paper. So less land is set aside for planting trees that will yield wood for paper, and other types of trees have room to grow naturally.

Being GREEN

If recycling programs are lacking in an area—start them! They help to reduce waste, save energy and resources, protect the environment, and also bring in money. Collecting and sorting plastics like PET and HDPE is especially helpful.

These "handy" seats are made from recycled PET.

29

Would you like your school, town, state, and country to lead the way, waste less, and recycle more? We can all help every day at home, school, and work, when shopping, and even while having fun.

LEAD THE WAY

We can persuade others to reduce waste, to reuse and recycle, and aim for a greener world. Why not design posters explaining how people can recycle different materials and put them up around your school?

FOR MORE INFORMATION

Organizations

THE COMPACT DISC RECYCLING CENTER OF AMERICA
68H Stiles Road
Salem, NH 03079
(603) 894-5553
Email:
info@cdrecyclingcenter.com
www.cdrecyclingcenter.com
Founded in 2006 to provide education, awareness, and options for CD and DVD recycling.

ENVIRONMENTAL PROTECTION AGENCY (EPA)
Ariel Rios Building
1200 Pennsylvania Avenue, NW
Washington, DC 20460
(202) 272-0167
www.epa.gov
The EPA is a federal government agency that identifies and tries to solve environmental issues and sets national standards.

FRIENDS OF THE EARTH
1717 Massachusetts Avenue, NW
Suite 600
Washington, DC 20036-2002
(202) 783-7400
Email: foe@foe.org
www.foe.org

The largest international network of environmental groups, campaigning for reduced levels of waste and more recycling.

NATIONAL RECYCLING COALITION, INC. (NRC)
805 15th Street, NW
Suite 425
Washington, DC 20005
(202) 789-1430
E-mail: info@nrc-recycle.org
www.nrc-recycle.org
The NRC is a national nonprofit advocacy group spanning all aspects of waste reduction, reuse, and recycling in North America.

THE NATURE CONSERVANCY
4245 North Fairfax Drive
Suite 100
Arlington, VA 22203-1606
(703) 841-5300
www.nature.org
The leading organization working around the world to protect ecologically important lands and waters for nature and people.

For further reading

Hewitt, Sally. *Waste and Recycling* (Green Team). New York, NY: Crabtree Publishing Company, 2008.

Hock, Peggy A. *Our Earth: Making Less Trash*. New York, NY: Children's Press, 2008.

Inskipp, Carol. *Reducing and Recycling Waste* (Improving Our Environment). Strongsville, OH: Gareth Stevens Publishing, 2005.

Orme, Helen. *Garbage and Recycling* (Earth in Danger). New York, NY: Bearport Publishing, 2008.

Silverman, Buffy. *Composting: Decomposition* (Do It Yourself). Chicago, IL: Heinemann, 2008.

Wilcox, Charlotte. *Earth-Friendly Waste Management* (Saving Our Living Earth). Minneapolis, MN: Lerner Publishing Group, 2008.

Web Sites

Due to the changing nature of Internet links, Rosen Publishing has developed an online list of Web sites related to the subject of this book. This site is updated regularly. Please use this link to access the list:
http://www.rosenlinks.com/pic/wast.

GLOSSARY

environment
The surroundings, including soil, rocks, water, air, plants, animals, and even human-made structures.

ferrous
A metal which contains mainly iron (scientific symbol Fe, "ferrum").

incinerator
A container for burning waste and garbage, usually at a very high temperature, leaving only ashes.

landfill site
An area of land where wastes are piled up and buried or covered.

leachate
Water that has soaked through an area, such as a landfill site, and gathered many chemicals and dissolved substances.

ore
Rocks or similar substances from the Earth which contain useful amounts of minerals or metals, such as iron, aluminum, or sulphur.

petroleum
Crude oil from the ground, often called oil, which is usually thick, dark, sticky – and very valuable.

pollutant
A substance that causes harm or damage to our surroundings, including to wildlife and to humans.

radioactivity
Rays of energy which are invisible but harmful to living things, including people, causing problems like sickness, burns, and cancers.

recycle
To use something again, or to take it apart or break it up, and use the substances it was made from again.

slag
Wastes and leftovers from mining valuable minerals such as coal, or from furnaces and incinerators.

toxic
Harmful, poisonous, or damaging to life.